Empathy/Caring for Others

Homesick Penguin

written and illustrated
by Ken Bowser

RED
CHAIR
•PRESS•

Please visit our website at **www.redchairpress.com**.
Find a free catalog of all our high-quality products for young readers.

 For a free activity page for this story, go to
www.redchairpress.com and look for Free Activities.

This book is dedicated to my grandson
Liam Hayden Bowser with love.

Homesick Penguin: Empathy/Caring for Others

Publisher's Cataloging-In-Publication Data
(Prepared by The Donohue Group, Inc.)

Bowser, Ken.

Homesick Penguin : empathy/caring for others / written and illustrated by Ken Bowser.
p. : col. ill. ; cm. -- (Funny bone readers)
Summary: Penguin likes to visit his friend Duck but he begins to miss some of the things
at home. How can Duck cheer up his homesick friend? This illustrated story shows young
readers the benefit of caring for the feelings of others. Book features: Big Words and Big
Questions.
Interest age level: 004-006.
ISBN: 978-1-939656-15-5 (lib. binding/hardcover)
ISBN: 978-1-939656-03-2 (pbk.)
ISBN: 978-1-939656-22-3 (ebook)
1. Caring--Juvenile fiction. 2. Homesickness--Juvenile fiction. 3. Penguins--Juvenile fiction.
4. Ducks--Juvenile fiction. 5. Caring--Fiction. 6. Homesickness--Fiction. 7. Penguins--Fiction.
8. Ducks--Fiction. I. Title.
PZ7.B697 Ho 2014

[E]   2013937167

This series first published by:
Red Chair Press LLC   PO Box 333   South Egremont, MA 01258-0333

Printed in the United States of America

1 2 3 4 5 18 17 16 15 14

Penguin lived in a faraway frozen place.

One day he went to visit his pal Duck.

Duck lived where it was very warm.

The next day, Penguin was sad.
Duck asked, "What is wrong?"

"I like visiting," said Penguin.
"But I miss my home."

7

Duck felt sorry for his friend.
He wanted to help.
"What can I do?" Duck wondered.

Suddenly Duck had an idea!
He grabbed his crayons and paints.

9

He collected books and magazines and lots of paper. Then, he began to draw.

10

Duck drew pictures of icebergs.
He drew whales and walruses.
He drew bears and birds.

He sketched seals and a sea lion.
He drew Penguin's home.

Duck even drew pictures of
some of Penguin's friends.

Duck found some tape.
Then he got a ladder.

15

Duck covered every wall with his pictures.
He even covered the ceiling.

When he had finished, Duck called
out to Penguin.
"Come inside, Penguin!" he said.

Penguin could not believe what he saw.

"I hope you feel more at home now,"
said Duck.
Penguin laughed. "I do!" he said.

Duck was a good friend.
He made Penguin feel very happy.
It made Duck very happy too.

When Penguin got home, he drew his own picture to thank his friend, Duck.

Big Questions: Why do you think Penguin was sad visiting his friend Duck? What did Duck do to make his friend feel better?

Big Words:

iceberg: large masses of ice floating in the sea

sketched: makes a rough or unfinished drawing

walrus: a big animal with tusks who lives in the Arctic